ALSO BY NA

Celebrity Crush Series

**MEET CUTE
OFF CAMERA**

The *Heroes and Villains* Series with Liza Penn:

**NEMESIS
ALTER EGO
SECRET SANCTUM
MAGICIAN
THUNDER
GODDESS**

Never miss a sexy release!
Join my mailing list:

https://rarebooks.substack.com/welcome

2

A Celebrity Crush Story

BESTSELLING AUTHOR
Natasha Luxe

4

CHAPTER ONE:
QUINN

The club is pulsing tonight, and so am I.

It's the same every time I get to a new shoot location. I'm disoriented, displaced; I need to connect, I need to *move*. Hitting the gym is only so effective—my body needs the push and heave of other bodies, the lot of us locked in one beating wave of energy that will root me to this new, foreign place.

Thank *god* this location isn't some middle of nowhere town. This location is close enough to a major city that in only twenty short minutes, we're pulling up at a club.

The base is heavy from behind the tall concrete walls. Not quite an LA club, no chic glowing lights or glitzy people waiting in a line. This city is all pull-them-up-by-your-bootstraps grit, with people stumbling for the doors in everything from short skirts and heels to jeans and tank tops.

I jump out of the car the moment Carmen parks. "We're done by midnight, got it?"

6

I have to bend back into the car.

Carmen's touching up her lipstick in the rearview mirror.

"Got it?"

"Yeah."

"7AM shoot, Car. *7AM.*"

"Yes, mom." Carmen rolls her eyes at me and tucks her lipstick back into her clutch. "You know that only gives us an hour and a half for any sort of fun?"

Yeah, I know. It's why I'm tapping my heeled foot on the concrete, my lips pursed at her, waiting.

She rolls her eyes again and finally climbs out of the rental car. "Okay, okay. Let's go."

The club may be far less glitz and glamor than I'm used to, but inside, it has the same energy. *Connection.* The heave and throb of dozens of strangers is linked by a pulsing, frantic beat. Alcohol flows from a bar off to the side, and that's where Carmen immediately goes—she drinks to wind down from the jetlag (even though we only traveled from LA to southern Oregon, but I won't point that out) while I head straight for the dance floor.

The music blares around me, the darkness interspersed with flashes of neon lights that cut a rainbow of colors through the fog. I *want* that fog, so I find the very center of the floor and close my eyes, letting my hands lift as the music builds.

The song breaks, and I fly.

One of the tips they give the crew to cope with constant travel is to find things you can keep the same no matter where you are. Create your own home on the road, so to speak. Most people choose things like eating the same breakfast or listening to the same white noise machine—but this is my constant. Leaping into the air, body thrashing back and forth, mind going blissfully blank so I'm *here*, fully *here*, in a totally entrancing way.

My constant wasn't always this.

But I learned my lesson the hard way: never make your constant a person.

The song bleeds into the next one and the crowd lets up a cheer, recognizing it, but I just move into it without breaking stride. Sweat starts to bead down my skin already, my heart throbbing in time to the music—

A hand snakes around my wrist. Carmen doesn't usually make it to the dance floor so soon.

But when I turn, it isn't Carmen.

8

Frustration sizzles through me. One of the biggest downfalls of *needing* this outlet is the guaranteed run-ins with dance floor scum. I never wear my faux engagement ring here, but maybe I should—I just don't like it's weight on my hand 24/7, reminding me of how very *faux* it is.

The guy holding my wrist gives a leer. In the flashing lights, it's hard to get a good look at him, but the energy he emits is instantly predatory.

I lurch back.

His grip holds.

The music drowns out my protest when I shout *No* and *Back off*.

His leer intensifies when he jerks me towards him and I crash into his body with a yelp. Before I can get away, his other arm tightens against me, keeping me pinned to him, and I writhe, but I can't get a fist up.

Panic starts to break through my delicious fog. Goddamn this man—*all* men, really.

Instead of grinding against me, he starts to walk us backwards, off the dance floor. I drop my heels into the floor, but he has at least a foot on me and a good hundred pounds. Carmen and I took a couple self-defense classes and I have mace in my clutch, but my mind is white with horror, with the wild look in the man's eyes that I catch in flashes of yellow light.

I start to scream when a fist comes sailing out of the darkness.

It smashes into the man's chin and he immediately drops his hold on me. I scramble back, mouth agape, to see a different guy already in the process of winding back for a second punch.

The first man doesn't come to his feet though. He lays on the floor, surrounded by still-dancing bodies, out cold.

Two other guys with flashlights charge towards us. Bouncers.

"What happened?" one shouts. His booming voice has no trouble being heard over the music.

I shake my head, my whole body starting to feel the aftereffects of fear. Cold sweats. Quaking muscles.

My savior starts to answer, his hands still in fists. The lights blare and retreat, pink and orange, dancing across him.

A surge of protection has me putting my hand on his chest.

"He drank too much," I shout at the bouncers, pointing at the unconscious guy. "Can't hold his liquor."

10

The bouncers eye me.

My savior does, too. He gives a half smile, realizing what I'm doing. If he tells them he knocked this creep out cold—however deservingly—they'll toss him from the club.

Other people are starting to notice now; the dancing is slowing around us. Bad for business.

The bouncers shrug. They bend to lift the unconscious man and drag him away.

"Thanks," my savior calls. He bends close to me, but not so close that it feels invasive. "You didn't have to do that."

"Neither did you," I shout back. It's hard to see him too well in this light, but what I can see has my body temperature launching back up. Smoky eyes, stubble shadowing his square jaw, and a fit, compact body under a striped button-up and jeans. His short brown hair is styled in a simple sweep back across his head, and he runs his hand through it now, his eyes dipping up and down my body quickly, not lingering like the now-unconscious creep.

I won't let one shitty encounter ruin my night. I want that energy back. I want my constant.

Heart racing already—the music is excellent here, really, all tight, fast beats and throbbing bases—I lean closer to the guy, brushing my lips over the shell of his ear. "Wanna dance?"

CHAPTER TWO:
SEBI

My eyes go wide. I fully expected this woman to disappear back into the crowd and find her friends, just take a minute to recuperate. A better guy would probably insist on it.

"Hell yeah, I want to dance," I say with a grin.

She smiles back at me, voluptuous lips in a dark shade that makes her look like an underworld goddess in this lighting. It's only offset by the brightness of her short blonde hair. Christ, this lighting looks far too *bedroom* suddenly. What would that hair look like splayed out on my pillow?

I shouldn't even be here at all. My agent and manager both would be flipping *shit*—I need to be back at my hotel, getting a good night's sleep before the shoot starts tomorrow. Nothing can get in the way of delaying this film, certainly not a hungover leading man. My agent had wanted me to back out on this project, but the director's

13

been a big supporter of me from the start—I can't disappoint him. So I'll get through this film—a spunky romantic comedy where I fall in love while making amends with my estranged dad—then jet off to start filming the movie that will define my career.

My stomach clenches at the thought. Christ, am I nervous? Maybe. Just a little. It's why I'm at a dance club the night before shooting starts. To go from quirky indie flicks and low-level films to a real big-budget, high-tech, name-recognition movie is the sort of career bump every actor dreams of.

So I can't fuck up this current film. I just gotta get through it.

Maybe I start to leave. Maybe I start to renege and tell the girl I have to get some sleep—

She grabs my hand and hauls me into the fray. Her thumb coasts over the knuckles that clocked out that guy, but honestly, the pain is gone. It'd been kind of fun to test out all those action moves I'm always practicing. No scene blocking here—this experience will help, I think. More authentic performance and what not.

Not that I want to run into more creeps. And the way this girl looks back at me over her shoulder as we hit the middle of the dance

14

floor has me wishing I could go find that unconscious shithead and beat him a few more times.

I'm not sure what to do with this unexpected swell of possessiveness, but I take her hips in my hands and press our bodies together, letting everyone around us know that she's dancing with me. No one else.

The beat rises. I make a mental note to ask the DJ for a set list later—I'm definitely adding this to my regulars. Maybe to my workout playlists. Or my sex playlists. Because, yeah, you gotta have at least one sex playlist, right? And the way this girl loops her arms around my neck as we jump with the crowd, swept up into the chaos whether we want to go or not—this song is all sex.

So is she.

Her tight little body is barely contained in the black dress she's wearing, her breasts swelling against the low neckline, the hem wrapped around the barest top of her thighs. All she'd have to do is bend over, and I could—

She spins around, pressing her ass back into my crotch. I'm hard—I've been hard since she touched my wrist—and I know she feels it. My hands stay on her waist, sliding

15

around to cup her belly, and I try, really, I do, to not reach too low, but then she jumps again, and my fingers brush her pussy through her dress.

I jump, too, because if I don't, I'll blow my load right then. The way this girl moves, every muscle in her body strung taut, her face relaxed in total euphoria, her curves hitting the beats and her limbs arching seductively—she has me on edge in five seconds flat. Holy fuck, how is this possible?

She leans back into me, her head falling over my shoulder, exposing her long neck.

I don't think. I can't. I'm action only, and my lips go to that skin, sweat-slick and glistening, and *Christ*, nothing has ever tasted so perfect. She's wearing some kind of vanilla perfume that shoots straight to my throbbing cock. Where else does she smell like this? Between her breasts? Her slit? Fuck, fuck—

Her body goes stiff momentarily, and I freeze too—I fucked up. This went too far. Shit.

But then she rocks her hips back into my hard-on again.

One of her hands reaches down, takes my wrist, and lifts it to palm her breast.

I hiss and my hand flexes on her boob, feeling her hard, pebbled nipple through the slinky fabric.

16

My lips climb to her ear. "Careful, doll. You're playing with fire."

Her lips curve into a grin that catches in a beam of blue light.

She spins again, coming face to face, and she kisses me right there on the dance floor. We may as well be alone—everyone is so wrapped up in their own dancing that two people making out is hardly exciting. Her tongue darts into my mouth and I moan against it, cradling the back of her head to go deeper, deeper. She returns with her own enthusiasm, one leg arching up to wrap around my thighs, pressing the heat of her pussy right over my erection.

Is she wearing panties?

Christ.

She spins again, and I'm left in a stumbling haze of painful arousal and aching confusion. I don't even know this girl. What the *fuck*. What the—

Her ass is against my crotch again. The music carries on, but suddenly the only thing I'm aware of is the way she's slowly pulling up the back of her dress.

I suck in a breath and plant my fingers into her hips. "What are you doing?" I growl into her ear.

She keeps going until her ass is bare, protected only by my crotch.

Then her fingers fumble at my belt buckle.

"Christ, doll—"

"Afraid to get caught?" She glances back at me with a grin so downright sexy, so tempting, that I forget rational language.

She. Wants me to fuck her. On the dance floor. Surrounded by dozens of people.

Oh my god.

Oh my *god*.

Her fingers work behind her back, undoing my belt, my fly. She reaches in, but I bat her fingers aside and work myself free as discreetly as I can. The darkness creates a cocoon around us, the press of bodies might as well be walls; so when I pull my dick out of my pants, it doesn't feel like I'm doing it in public.

Thank god I always have a condom in my pocket. This is why. This is absolutely why.

I roll it on as I slide my other hand down her ass—she's not wearing panties, naughty girl—and I find her slit by feel. She's scorching hot, and her tight folds close greedily around my fingers, sucking me in up to the knuckle.

A gasp yanks out of my throat. My dick is wet with pre-cum—I need to be inside her, need it *now*.

18

While I work for the best angle, I loop my arm around her front and slip my fingers up under her dress. Her clit is swollen already and when I touch it, she throws her head back against my shoulder, her body limp, mine for the taking.

My cock finds her entrance.

The music rises, rises—

When it breaks, the dancers scream, and I shove into her. The girl cries out, her pleasure lost in the masses, and when the beat sets off thumping, I move in time with it.

She's so fucking tight. Her walls ripple upward, drawing me deeper, deeper, every muscle in her pussy enfolding my dick in her warm wetness. Electric sensations flit into my balls, begging for release, but I refuse to go until she does, until she screams out into the club.

My fingers work that clit, rubbing in smooth circles that follow the sway of the music. I want my tongue there; I want to taste her; I settle for licking her neck, biting her earlobe, sucking it into my mouth.

"This is what I'll be doing to that hot little clit of yours," I say into her ear. "I'm going to get you some place where I can fuck you properly. You like my cock inside you?"

I thrust, and she nods, her eyelids fluttering, her face contorted in the building ecstasy of impending orgasm.

"I'm gonna come," she gasps, and I barely just read the words on her lips. "I'm gonna—"

I take her clit between my thumb and finger and pinch it.

She screams. The music swells, swallowing it, and I follow her over the edge, cursing into her neck as my dick unloads inside her, balls squeezing tight. I brace her hips and rock hard into her, and she cries out again, those tight muscles shuddering around my cock.

We come down from it together, swaying gently, though the music is still rough and fast.

She's the one who pulls herself together first—she eases forward and slides her dress back into place. I grab my dick and stuff it into my pants, condom and all. But she doesn't go far; she twists, wrapping her arms around my neck, and then her mouth is on mine again, a slower, luxurious kiss as she traces my jaw with her thumb.

Oh my god.

Who the fuck is this girl?

I'm in love. There's no other word for it.

20

I'd punch out a hundred creeps for her; I'd follow her to the ends of the earth.

"Your name," I mumble into her mouth. "Your number. I need to see you again."

She grins. Did she hear me? Fuck this music.

I bend to her ear. "I need to see you again."

She kisses my neck and mimes getting a drink. She wants a drink? I'll get her one of everything at this bar.

But when I start after her, she waves me off. "I'll be back," she mouths.

I don't want her out of my sight.

Her eyes drop to my crotch. Oh. Yeah. I should probably take care of that.

I point toward the bathrooms then shout, "I'll meet you at the bar."

She bites her lip in a grin, and oh my god, yep, I'm in love.

I race through the crowd and clean up in the bathroom in two seconds flat. My heart thunders, or maybe it's the music, or maybe it's my body realizing I just fucked the most gorgeous girl on a dance floor, and this is it, this is the pinnacle of happiness.

Back out on the main floor, I hurry to the bar.

The only people there are a few couples, one lone guy.

I scan the area. Elbows like battering rams, I dive into the dancers, but none are *her*, that bright hair, that lithe body.

When I stumble out by the entrance, my heart sinks into my toes.

She's gone.

CHAPTER THREE: QUINN

It's hours later, the sun has risen, I'm at *work*, for fuck's sake, but all I can think about is that guy.

I don't even know his name.

It's a small town, though. Surely someone at the club would know him if I went back and asked around—which would *totally defeat the purpose of running out on him, hello.*

I groan and take another swig of coffee. Not enough on the planet for this morning. I'm not hungover, thank god—Carmen has *that* consequence locked down—but I'm...can you be hungover from sex?

My body still ripples with pleasure at every memory of his touch. The expert way he'd fingered my clit, then taken it between his fingers right as I was coming to pull the orgasm through every part of my body like a whipping tornado. The sheer length of his cock, battering my walls, hitting my G-spot exactly right...

Another gulp of coffee.

23

Fuck me. That is *not* part of my constant. Sure, I'll find the occasional one-night stand; but never *on the dance floor.* What the fuck came over me?

"You ready?" My boss, Theresa, peeks her head in the makeup trailer.

"Yeah, yeah. You get Carmen's text?"

Theresa sighs. "Hungover on the first day. New record for her."

"She'll be back tomorrow."

"Uhuh. Left you to clean up her mess?"

"It's fine." I pull out her notes for her client. "I'll get my guy done, then move onto hers. Shouldn't be a problem."

"You're a goddess, Quinn," Theresa calls and lets the door shut after her.

I know, I know.

I'd felt like one last night. A goddess of sex.

I groan in the empty trailer and toss Carmen's notes down two stations. I haven't even looked at her client yet. She got the leading man for this film; I'm on the supporting cast, which for this first day of shooting is just the main character's father. Simple styling, minimal makeup, basic old man get-up.

24

He comes in promptly at 7AM, and I'm all too eager to throw myself into work. The guy's hot, for sure; all actors are in their own ways, especially ones cast in films like this, a romantic comedy feel-good film.

But I see him note my ring. The rock glints in the light, sparkles like a firecracker, and after that, our conversation is strictly companionable.

That's why I kept wearing it, even after...everything.

The ring is my savior. My *closed for business* sign.

I should've worn it last night.

Shouldn't I have?

I had sex with a complete stranger in the middle of a crowd of people.

Once Carmen sobers up, I have to talk to her about it. I have to talk to *someone* about it.

"All set," I tell the client. "Send in the next guy, would you?"

He nods his thanks and kicks his way out of the trailer. I hear the door open again a beat later and footsteps pad in, but I'm bent over Carmen's notes, trying to get my brain to focus on her writing.

The actor's name: Sebastian Stanik. Minimal makeup, check. Basic hair styling for this scene. Easy enough.

The next client sits in the chair behind me.

As I turn to face him, I flip the notes over to get a glimpse of his head shot.

My whole body goes stiff. Head to toe. I'm encased in stone.

Holy shit. Holy *fucking* shit.

I'm having a stroke.

Because it's *him* in that headshot.

The guy who, not twelve hours ago, had his dick in my pussy. Sure, the lights were low and flashing, and I wasn't exactly *facing* him a whole lot. But that's *him.*

I lower the paper and look at the guy sitting in my chair.

He stays reclined, wearing dark sunglasses, earbuds in, jaw propped in one hand. He looks exhausted, but the moment I show my face, he comes wide awake.

He rips the glasses off his face and yanks out an earbud.

I can hear a song thumping from it. Is that…is that the song we fucked to last night?

"Oh my god," he says. "*You.*"

He launches up from the chair and advances on me, but he stops when I stay stiff.

26

He *is* hot. I'd thought so in the club's darkness, but now, in the bright white lights of the trailer, it's undeniable. His broad shoulders stretch his tight blue t-shirt, muscular legs showing from beneath loose basketball shorts. Those soft gray eyes are all innocent and open, staring at me like he wants to fall to his knees at my feet. He drops his sunglasses to the counter and shoves both earbuds into his pockets, and once his hands are free, his fingers clench and unclench, fighting reaching for me, and I might let him, all I need to do is smile, and he'll dive in—

But then his eyes, those innocent, happy eyes, drop to my hand.

And he flares backwards.

"You're *married*?"

CHAPTER FOUR: SEBI

I *knew* there was a catch. I fucking knew it. It was too perfect, right? Too goddamn perfect.

My dream girl is married to someone else. Someone else gets to have her in their bed each night. Someone else gets that tight pussy, those euphoric rippling muscles, that warm little clit—

"Holy Christ." I drop back onto the chair because the only other option is to sprint out the door, and I am not a runner, goddammit.

The girl stares at me like she's still trying to process me. I sure as hell didn't expect to see her either, but I get a little bit more reason to be *shocked*, don't I?

When she goes a full minute without saying anything, I splay my hands wide.

"What the *fuck*?" I ask, but it comes out pained because I spent all night thinking of her, worrying some creep had come and made off with her. I'd barely slept at all and planned to go back to the club after the scene wraps

28

today to ask around for her. Small town and all, someone would know who she is. The DJ hadn't had a clue, but he'd been good enough to get me his set list, and I'd been listening to that techno song on repeat all night.

Only it turns out that she and I are both part of the same film crew, who both happened to go to the same club to blow off steam the night before shooting.

I'd think it was fate if not for that *fucking rock on her hand*.

Finally, she shivers, and comes out of her shock enough to look down at her finger.

"Oh," she moans to it, rubbing her forehead.

"Yeah."

"It's not what it looks like."

"Well, it *looks* like you made an ass out of me and whoever you're married to. What kind of person does that? Wait—was that guy I punched *your husband?*"

"No! I'm not—" She plants her palms over her face. When she brings them down, her eyes are bloodshot. "I'm not married, okay?"

All the fury in my body pauses. "Say that again?"

She licks her lips. The movement reawakens that initial surge I'd felt when I saw her moments ago—relief, joy, and a tight winding of arousal.

"This ring isn't real," she says. Why does she look like she's about to cry? "I just wear it while I'm on the job to prevent…unwanted advances. I don't date actors."

I launch back up from the makeup chair. When I close the space between us, she sips in a breath, but doesn't move away.

Christ, she still smells amazing. That vanilla hint that makes my insides flip. It's impossible to hide my growing hard-on in these basketball shorts, but I don't want to. Let her see it; let it torture her a bit like she's been torturing me.

"No," I tell her. "Say that again. The part where you said you aren't married."

Her eyebrows peak. "I'm…not married?"

"Again. Not as a question."

Her eyes flare with the softest hint of annoyance at my command. "I'm not married."

I exhale, long and loud, and brace one hand on either side of her, pinning her to the makeup table. "Doll, you *wrecked* me, you know that?"

She has her hands behind her, her breasts stretching the fabric of her simple white sundress. It's lacey and flirty and so fucking hot, and now that I know she's not taken, I want to rip it off her body and punish her for tormenting me so much.

My relief is so overwhelming that I run my nose up the side of her neck, needing to touch her in some small way. She makes a startled chirp but doesn't push me off, and I can smell the building arousal on her, a heat that has her rubbing her legs together.

"Here I thought there was someone else touching this body," I say into her jaw. "I was imagining someone else's fingers here—" I lay my hand on her stomach, just a hint of a touch inches above her pussy. "—and someone else's mouth on your skin. Do you have any idea how much pain you put me through, doll?"

She trembles against me. For all the confidence she exuded last night, she's remarkably restrained now, her head tipped to the side, her face pinched like she's fighting her desire, fighting the urge to throw herself on me.

"Last night," she manages, her voice low and coarse, "was a mistake."

I chuckle, tracing my lips back down her neck where I nudge aside the strap of her dress until it trickles down her arm. "A mistake? Is that why you left?"

"Yes. I shouldn't have—" She yanks in a breath when my teeth lightly bite down on the apex of her shoulder. "I don't usually do that."

"Good. I don't want to imagine you fucking anyone else, remember?" In a flash, I swipe my hands under the backs of her thighs and plop her down on the edge of the makeup table. She anchors on my shoulders, eyes closed, brows pinched, but she doesn't do anything to protest. In fact, she leans into me, her cheek pressing to mine so I feel her hot breath burst on the bend of my neck.

Her head tips backward and I see her warring for control. Whatever game of reasoning she's playing with herself, I have to win—she may not see it yet, but last night wasn't a mistake. Not in any way. It *was* fate. This kind of chemistry doesn't come along every day. Fuck, she gets me hard just with a look—touching her, my lips on something as innocent as her shoulder, and I could come.

And I still don't even know her fucking name.

32

I pull my earbuds out of my pocket. The song is still going—it'll keep playing on repeat until I stop it—and I put one bud in her ear, one in mine.

Her eyes flash open. Her pupils go huge, and I see the change in her—she's transported back to last night. Suddenly we're on that dance floor again. That's what I love about music and the right carefully cultivated playlist—it can set a scene like nothing else.

The beat throbs between us and my fingers glide down the front of her dress. I slowly peel up the hem of her skirt and my fingertips part the edge of her panties to delve into the soft, warm folds where they were last night.

She sucks in a breath, her breasts heaving towards me, and I cannot be this lucky—this cannot be real, that I found this girl again.

Christ help me, she's as wet as I am hard, and I ease three fingers into her no problem.

I finger-fuck her slowly, building up pleasure that has her moaning softly and rocking side to side as I lower to my knees between her splayed legs.

"Tell me your name," I whisper, my lips on her the inside of her thigh.

The music hits a crescendo.

"Quinn," she says. "Quinn McGill."

"Quinn," I repeat. "My Quinn, my doll."

I bend forward and run one long lick up the center of her folds. Christ, she tastes delicious, all sultry and sweet, and I can't help but lick her again, again, devouring every inch of her pussy. She curves up in a sharp buck, a small, keening cry echoing through the trailer. I don't have a condom, but I'm having plenty of fun with my fingers and tongue in her pussy. The little frustrated moans and delicious whimpers she makes are the sweetest sounds I've ever heard, but I want to ease them at the same time—I slide my fingers back into her pussy and alternate thrusts in time with the pulse of the music as I trap her clit with my tongue. That little nub is already swollen, so goddamn responsive that I moan into her.

There's a knock on the trailer door.

Shit, shit—

"Sebastian?" A voice calls. "Ten minutes til rolling."

Quinn rocks back from me hard enough to slam into the mirror. "Fuck. Fuck! Stop, we have to—"

34

I launch to my feet, gasping for breath as much as she is. She leans against the mirror, fighting to compose herself, her eyes tightly shut, and I'd give anything to hear what's going through that gorgeous head.

"Quinn," I try, wiping her juices from my chin. She didn't come, and the disappointment settles in my chest. I need to make her come; I need her writhing around me, completely satisfied. "Talk to me."

She eases the earbud out and sets it on the counter next to her.

"It was a *mistake*," she says again, and my heart cracks. She opens her eyes, but she won't look at me, quickly smoothing her skirts back over her thighs. "I told you—I don't date actors. Now…get in the chair. I need to get you ready."

"They'll wait."

"The fuck they will! It'll be my ass on the line."

She's right. Of course she's right. I need this movie to run on time, too, but all I want in this moment is to give her the orgasm she deserves.

I pop out my earbud and drop to the chair. I try to catch her attention in the mirror, but she busies herself at a table of makeup powders, her fingers shaking.

"Quinn—"

35

"Just stop, okay? It didn't happen. We won't talk about it. As far as you know, I'm just your makeup artist. I won't even be after today—I'm just filling in for Carmen. So let's just get through today, and then we can carry on our merry way, all right?"

My eyes flip to my own reflection and I see cheeks flushed red from watching Quinn's beautiful body pulse in ecstasy. Her cheeks are as red as mine.

She's attracted to me. I can feel it; she can feel it.

"You don't date actors," I echo what she'd said. "That's your only hang-up?"

She doesn't reply. Her lips purse into a tight line and she fumbles with a jar of concealer.

I grin, cocky, confident, and twist in the chair.

"Look at me, Quinn."

She rolls her eyes. After a long pause, she finally does, and when her gaze meets mine, I can see how hard she's fighting her self-imposed rules.

"I'm not just an actor," I tell her.

"Yes, you are. You all are."

All? Hm.

"I'm not," I say. "And I'll prove it to you."

36

She huffs and turns away. "No. You won't."

"I will. And—" I wait until she turns back. Then I run my thumb over my chin and stick it in my mouth. "You'll need to clean yourself off of me, doll. You were soaked. I plan to finish what I started there, too."

Her whole face turns red. She grabs a stack of wipes and chucks them at me.

My grin doesn't quit. There's nothing I like more than a challenge. And if the prize is convincing my doll that whatever fears she has are safe with me? Then I'll more than rise to it.

CHAPTER FIVE:
QUINN

This is *hell*. Pure and utter fucking *torture*.

Carmen is coherent enough by the time I get back to the hotel that I tell her everything, every sordid detail, from the dance floor sex to Sebastian being in my makeup chair this morning.

And she *howls*.

She laughs so hard that her neighbor in the hotel pounds on the wall. I have a bolt of horror wondering if Sebastian is in one of these rooms, but no—they put the actors in the swankier hotel up the street. Didn't they? They did. They had to. Fate isn't *that* cruel.

"Oh my *god*, Quinn! You fucked Sebastian Stanik! *In public!*"

"Stop! God, can't you see how messed up this is?"

"Messed up in the best way, you mean?"

"*No*, I mean *messed up,* messed up. He's an actor."

That sobers her. "Quinn, it's been a year. Maybe—"

38

"Don't say it. Don't even try to convince me that in the past year, actors have all miraculously gotten less self-absorbed. I mean, what kind of person fucks a girl on a dance floor, in public, without knowing her name?"

"Um, *you* did that. What kind of person are you?"

I groan and lob a pillow at her. "You're not helping. Thank god you'll have him tomorrow. I'm not—"

"Oh-ho-ho, Quinn my darling, *definitely* not." Carmen whips out her phone and starts clacking a text.

I leap up from the couch and hurl myself at her on the bed, but she dodges, hits send.

"There. I just told Theresa to swap our clients. *You* get the leading guy, *I* get the supporting, and we *all* go home happy, eh?"

"You asshole!" I grab the pillow I threw and smack her with it, feeling all the blood in my body rush to my face. "Why the fuck would you do that?"

"Because I love you, you idiot. You've been locked in your dumb rules for too long—this will do you some good. Besides, you do realize I just gave you a *promotion*, right?"

I pause mid-swing, up on my knees beside her.

Oh.

She really did.

Being able to put that I was Sebastian Stanik's stylist on my resume will definitely not suck. He's one of the hottest up and coming actors—Carmen had been giddy to work with him for her own resume, and because, as she'd said, he's a *total babe*.

She's not wrong.

At all.

And I hate her for it.

"Goddammit, Car." I sink to the bed. My heart won't slow down. My cheeks hurt, they're so hot.

She grins at me. "I love you too, you dumbass."

The next morning, I'm absolutely dreading being in that trailer. The only thing that gets me in there is knowing Carmen will be there the whole time, too, so Sebastian and I won't have the temptation of being alone.

My god, I can never be alone with him ever again. My body has completely shucked my *no dating actors* rules; my clit is still swollen and throbbing from his tongue yesterday, frustrated arousal making me grouchy as I slam open makeup trays and spread out supplies.

40

Carmen watches me, smirking the whole time.

Our clients come in together, the same two I had yesterday. Sebastian goes right to me, not even bothering to see if Carmen and I switched; he just sits in my chair and beams up at me.

I glance at Carmen, who is totally checking out her guy as he bends over to fix his jeans cuff. He's got to be at least twice her age, but yeah, I see the appeal.

She looks back at me and mouths *Thank you.*

It makes me grin.

So when I turn back to Sebastian, smiling, his whole face changes. The teasing glint in his eye fades and the muscles in his cheeks relax.

"My mission in life," he says, "is to make you smile like that again."

I roll my eyes and step behind him. "Good luck."

"Ah, doll, I don't need luck. I have chemistry."

"Can't build a relationship on chemistry."

"I agree." He pulls out his phone. I think he's going to ask for my number—big *nope*—but he just finds the Notes app and clears his throat.

41

"Question One: Where were you born?" he asks as I dab concealer on my finger.

I tip his chin up and start smoothing it under his eyes. His gaze locks with mine, and I'm suddenly aware of how intimate a position this is. Usually I whip through it so fast that I don't have time to linger on how I'm barely a few inches away from clients, but now—I inhale, and I smell his mint toothpaste and a burst of woodsy cologne.

My finger slows. I'm stroking the soft skin under his eyes and my thumb drops down, runs along the line of stubble that cuts through his cheek.

Why does touching him so feel natural? I'm mesmerized by the feel of his skin, soft and muscular, and the roughness of his stubble.

He clears his throat.

I jerk away, coughing to the makeup cart. "Why do you care where I was born?"

God, I'm amazed I remembered what he asked.

I hear the smile in his voice as he goes, "I'm trying to get to know you, Quinn. They're easy questions, anyway. Consider it small talk. Look, those two are talking."

42

Sebastian points at Carmen and the dad-actor, who are indeed talking, Carmen giggling.

I sigh. "Fine. I was born in southern Cali. Born and bred."

There's a pause. "You're not going to ask me where I was born?"

"I know where you were born." I grab some powder foundation. "The whole internet does. Eastern Europe, right?"

Sebastian glances up at me. Is he blushing? Why is that sexy?

Then he parts those lips and purrs something in a language I don't recognize, all rough syllables but rolling consonants.

Everything in my body turns to molten liquid.

Oh, fuck, that's just not even fair.

"Yes, doll," he translates, one corner of his mouth in a cocky grin. "Eastern Europe. Does that mean you Googled me?"

"I did not—"

"Question Two." He turns to his phone with an infuriating smirk. I want to kiss it off his face.

Fuck, no I do *not*.

I hurriedly brush the foundation over his face, not pausing to get lost in touching him again.

"Favorite ice cream flavor?" he asks.

"Can't have dairy."

"Ah, good to know. Favorite food?"

I grab the pomade and start working it into his hair. The moment my fingers run through it, I inadvertently pull my lower lip into my mouth, sucking once.

He sees me in the mirror.

Our eyes connect, and for one full, idiotic breath, I hold that gaze.

I imagine grabbing his hair.

Pulling it.

Screaming his name.

God fucking damn it.

"Sushi," I say.

Sebastian blinks. "What?"

"My favorite food. Sushi."

He drops his eyes to his phone. The screen has gone dark. "Ah. Yeah. Right."

His voice sounds gruff, heady. It makes me tighten my legs together, and I spin to the table of supplies just to catch my breath.

This isn't good.

This is really, really not good.

I know how this ends.

But when I turn back to him, any resolve I think I have evaporates, and we spend the next twenty minutes bantering questions back and forth. Inane things,

44

favorite city we've worked in—mine, Austin; his, Berlin, which is unfair because I haven't done abroad yet—career goals—mine, to keep getting steady jobs; his, the same, remarkably, despite his rising success—family—mine, mom and dad in southern Cali still; his, mom in Pennsylvania.

By the time he leaves the trailer with a wink and a promise to see me later, I rock back against the table, and curse myself over and over again.

He did it. He really did manage to make me see him as *more than an actor*. Which is exactly why I wear the ring that I…totally forgot to put on today. But when I *do* wear it, it keeps everyone at arm's length, never letting me get to this point of seeing them beyond the job.

I really can't tell if it's still as scary as it should be, or if maybe, just maybe, I like this guy too much to care.

CHAPTER SIX:
SEBI

I can't wait until tomorrow to see Quinn again. I think my questions broke through to her, but she's more stubborn than anyone I've ever met—who knows what she could convince herself about us in all that time?

So I rush over to the makeup trailer right after the scene wraps. And there she is, walking for the crew's hotel shuttle with her friend, Carmen.

"Quinn!" I jog up to her.

She turns, her eyes widening at the sight of me. The rest of the crew turns as well, and yeah, okay, it *is* always a bit of a scandal when actors crossover and date the crew—but Christ, I can't help it. This girl has me absolutely obsessed, and I don't care that everyone sees it. My agent and manager might, but they're back in LA, and I feel strangely like my parents aren't here to chastise me.

Quinn waves Carmen to keep going and grabs my arm, pulling me out of the line for the bus.

46

"What are you doing here?"

"Trying something," I admit. "Will you go out with me tonight?"

She hesitates. And then, expectedly, though it guts me, she shakes her head.

"I don't date—"

"Actors. I know." But I smile. "So don't."

"What?"

"I don't want to date you," I tell her. "Let's not date. Let's just have sex."

"What?" It comes as a sharp laugh.

Christ, that laugh. She's hypnotic.

"Let's just have sex." I step closer to her, shading her body with mine as the sun sets far behind me. "And if we get to know each other between rounds, so be it. But it isn't dating."

"Sebastian—"

"Call me Sebi."

She gives me a flat stare and god help me, I think I love her annoyance almost as much as I love her happiness. "Sebi," she echoes, and it goes straight to my dick, hard against my jeans. "I don't think that's a good idea."

"Oh, it's a terrible idea," I admit. "But I'm out of reasons to keep my hands off you. I left you hanging yesterday, and I know that body is aching to release, isn't it?" I drop my voice low, letting one hand come up to brush along her bare arm. A shiver makes her twitch, goosebumps erupting across her skin. "I promised I'd make it up to you. Let me put my tongue back on that clit, doll. I need to taste you again."

"God, Sebi—" Quinn rocks towards me. She has to brace herself with a hand on the center of my chest, and I capture it, holding it there.

"Feel my heart going crazy? That's for you. Only you. Come to my hotel room. Put us both out of our misery, just for one night."

She groans, low and exasperated, and I know I have her. I know she's mine.

Her fingers fist in the fabric of my shirt. "One night."

We get a car to my hotel, a block over from hers, and it takes everything in me not to jump her in the backseat.

She's wearing a sundress again—Christ save me from her flirty little dresses—and I note that she hasn't worn that ring since yesterday. Is she no longer trying to prevent my advances? It'd have driven me crazy if she kept wearing it.

The car stops on the curb and I hop out, then reach in to help her.

48

She gives me an odd look. "Gentlemanly."

"Hardly. I have dark ulterior motives."

"Ah, some truth!"

"I've been nothing but truthful, doll. As I always will be." I lead her into the lobby, past the bar, where most of the other upper crew and cast are already flocking.

A few spot me with surprise when they see Quinn on my arm. I'm not known for one-night stands. My two main costars for my next film, the big budget one, are always splayed across the tabloids with various girls. Chris Griffins is my age and has a reputation that would make my manager faint with stress; Garth Daniels is about a decade older, a Hollywood staple, and he seems to collect marriages like baseball cards. While I'll admit at least Chris's lifestyle is a bit tempting, my heart's just never been in it.

Until Quinn. And now, my heart's all the way fucking in. I don't think she understands just how rare this is for me. Maybe that's the problem—she expects me to be like Chris or Garth or any of the other self-absorbed guys she's worked with.

The elevator opens for us and, thank god, it's empty.

The moment the doors close, I feel Quinn eye me.

"I really don't do this," I tell her.

She frowns. "Do what?"

"This." I wave at us. "I don't *fuck around*, as they say. So if you're worried you're a trophy for me—"

"Aren't I?"

The way her eyes narrow, as though it's obvious, makes me wince.

"You have a history with actors," I say. It isn't exactly something she's kept secret, but she's definitely avoided any specifics in that area.

The elevator pings. We get off, and I lead her down the hall. The air between us tightens the closer we get to my room, and I worry our conversation will derail.

But she leans her shoulder on the wall as I fish for my key. "That ring wasn't always fake."

I go perfectly still. "You *were* married."

She nods. "Annulled almost a year ago. It was a dumb rushed thing. We never should have—" She sucks in a breath. Holds it. "I should have seen the signs."

"Such as?" I don't open the door. Not yet. I don't want this conversation to sully our moments alone.

50

Quinn holds my eyes and I see hers tear. I reach for her, gathering her hands and pulling them to my chest.

"Lack of attention," she says. "Interest fading almost immediately after we fucked for the first time. But he proposed, and I didn't see it for what it was: a publicity stunt." She shrugs one shoulder. "We didn't even last a week after the shotgun wedding."

"Oh, doll." I cup her jaw in my hand. Hearing how this trash treated Quinn, like she was some prop to be used to gain media attention…

I press my lips to hers, hovering there, just letting her feel my breath on her skin, feel my presence with her. "I know you know this, but he's a fool, Quinn. An absolute fucking moron for not realizing how special you are."

She laughs once, short, disbelieving. "Yeah, okay. You just want in my pants."

"Yes. But I believe it, too. And if you like, we can spend all of tonight with me just describing, in delicate, precise details, exactly how perfect each part of your body and soul is." I kiss the side of her mouth and pull her hips square with mine. "Especially your body. I may linger over a few descriptions—"

"Open the *door*," she pleads, her voice teasing, and I revel in seeing her smile, the light in her eyes returned.

I obey, but my mind is still reeling. So this is why she's so hesitant to trust me, her secret revealed. She's worried I'll use her for my own game, then dump her the moment I get what I need.

But what I need is her. In every way, for as long as she wants. *She's* the one in control here.

I have to show her that.

I guide her into the room and pop on the light. It's a nice suite, with a wide main room and a huge king bed. The bathroom has both a shower and a jacuzzi tub, and while I'd hoped to make quick use of that tub with her, I turn to Quinn and take her hands again.

"Doll," I say, holding her gaze, letting her see my earnestness. "I was serious. We don't have to have sex tonight. If you want to just—"

"I thought that's what this was," she cuts me off. "Just sex. No dating."

I wince. "Okay. That may have been a lie."

"You said you'd always tell the truth?"

"I really did intend to just have sex with you. But…" I run my hand through my hair. "I may not be capable of it."

52

"Ah. So you…lured me to your hotel room with promises of fucking, but your evil master plan was to date me? That seems backwards."

She smiles, so I do, too.

"Well. When you put it that way."

"Sebi." She takes a deep breath and steps closer to me. Her eyes flutter shut. "I think all I can handle right now is sex. The rest is just…too much."

I kiss her cheekbone. "I will take whatever you can give me, doll. If you give me your body, I will worship it. If you feel safe enough to give me your heart one day, I will protect it. You're the one in control, Quinn. You make the choices. And you can leave, too, if that's what you want."

I hold there, praying she doesn't pick the latter. Christ, let her stay, in some way, let her choose to stay with me.

Quinn holds against me, her eyes shut.

Finally, she breaks them open to look up at me.

She presses up onto her toes and hooks her mouth with mine.

CHAPTER SEVEN: QUINN

I'm in control.

That's certainly a first. In every area. With my career, always hoping and praying I get another job, another film. With my relationships, always hoping and praying the guy I'm with chooses to text back, to schedule another date, to not fucking *leave me*.

But I know this relationship with Sebi is doomed from the start—the film ends in, what, a few weeks? And he'll be off to whatever shoot is next, while I head back to LA and wait for the next assignment. So since I can go in knowing that, maybe I can let this be what it is: a fling.

Because, I'll be honest—I want this man's body. I *need* his body. I need it fully, not mostly clothed on a dance floor. I need his mouth back on my clit.

So that's what it will be. Sex, mind-blowing, leg-shaking sex, and then we go our separate ways, no feelings hurt.

54

I reach for the zipper at the side of my dress and shimmy out of it. It pools around my feet, showing Sebi that while I'm wearing underwear, I'm braless.

This is the first time, I realize, that he's seeing me naked.

A flush climbs my neck as his eyes drop over my body. My nipples tighten, but I'm far from cold—everything feels too hot, too raw.

Sebi's cheeks turn pink. I've noticed that about him, that the edges of his cheekbones tend to flare bright red the moment his emotion intensifies.

"Christ, doll," he whispers. He starts to reach for me but yanks back, his eyes widening with mischief. "Oh! Hang on, one sec."

My eyebrows peak as he spins to a desk and pushes a button on a…is that a speaker system?

A beat later, I see him scrolling through playlists. He taps one.

"Does that say *Sex Playlist?*" I can't help but laugh.

He turns back with a wicked grin. "You'll thank me."

"You have a sex playlist." Another laugh bubbles up, easing whatever remaining uncertainty I had.

"*Everything's* better with the right playlist, doll."

The first song starts.

It's the one we fucked to in the club. Fast beats, throbbing and writhing and—yeah, okay, this is setting a mood for sure.

I laugh again, hands to my mouth, dissolving in giggles, and Sebi dives in, sweeping me into his arms. My breasts press against his shirt, rubbing the sensitive skin as our lips meet, smile folding over smile.

He walks me backwards and drops me onto the bed, my breasts bouncing.

"I'm going to kiss every part of you," he says, keeping his mouth on mine. "I don't want there to be a single inch of your skin without a memory of my lips on it."

God, this guy and his words. Is it a line from a film? Fuck, I don't even care.

He climbs onto the bed over me, easing me onto my back, our lips locked. My fingers grab for his shirt and I heft it over his head—oh, *save me*, he's ripped. Of course he is; this movie has no small amount of shirtless scenes, and his abs and pecs reflect that, utterly defined.

I run my fingers through the divots across his stomach, tracing a line down to the trail of hair that leads below his belt.

"I want to see your body," I tell him.

He shudders as I work his belt. "You have it, doll. You have all of me."

That sounds an awful lot like relationship-speak, but I don't care. My body temperature is skyrocketing, my nipples erect to the point of pain.

I pull open his belt, his fly, and he kicks his pants and boxers off, and *fuck*.

I'd known he was sizable at the club. His length had easily slid into me and stayed in despite standing like we were, and each thrust had pressed directly on my G-spot. But seeing it now, his cock is long and thick, curved up slightly, and I know my panties are soaked when I curl my fingers around his dick.

"Condom," I pant. "Now."

"Are you sure?" He kisses my ear and ghosts his lips down my neck. "I have some kissing to do first."

I sip in a gasp as he grabs a nipple in his mouth.

"Okay, okay, maybe the condom can wait."

His tongue flips against my hard nipple while he pinches the other, and I rock back into the bed, moaning, the pleasure-pain building almost to a breaking point.

The music softens, a misleading lull, and then *bursts*.

He twists his fingers, and I babble a cry.

"Christ, your breasts are sensitive," he says, his lips dipping to the top of my belly.

"Yeah, a little," I manage between gulps of air.

He grins up at me. "I'll remember that."

I'm very quickly forgetting why I resisted this man at all.

His kisses walk down my belly, and he draws a line across my hips with his tongue. I shiver, arching up into it. Fuck, he isn't even down to my clit yet, and I know I'm drenched.

His thumbs hook my underwear, yank them off. I splay my thighs for him and he chuckles, giving a tentative lick at the very top of my thigh.

"So eager for me, are you, doll?" He presses a single finger into my slit and pulls it out, the tip glistening. "So fucking eager. Christ, look how wet you are. Did we stain that dance floor? Does everyone in town know exactly what you let me do to you?"

"Yes," I pant, all helpless gasps. "Yes, they do."

"Fuck right, they do," he says, and then his mouth is on my clit.

I cry out as the sharp edge of his tongue swipes against my sensitive nub. He shoves three fingers into my cunt, sawing them in and out in time to the music.

I'm embarrassed by how close I already am. Pleasure wrenches tight, the muscles in my belly and down my thighs twisting tight, tighter—

He reaches up, keeping his mouth on my clit, and tweaks my nipples, one in each hand.

"Oh god, Sebi—don't stop—" I'm a mess, blubbering, begging.

He licks harder, faster, his tongue viciously set on my clit as his fingers twist and squeeze the very tips of my nipples.

The music swells and something about the tempo yanks my orgasm out rough and fast. I come with a sharp scream, waves roiling up my chest and down to my toes, leaving me thrashing as his tongue milks out the last ripples.

I grab his arms and drag him up to me, suctioning my lips to his. I taste myself on him, in the crevices of his mouth, and he plunges that tongue inside with abandon.

The song switches. I don't recognize it, but I don't need to—my body reacts, bending up to meet his, my blood pulsing in my veins, my heart thundering behind my ribs.

"I need you," I beg into his mouth. "I need you inside of me, Sebi, *now*, please—"

"Christ, beg for me, doll," he whimpers and sucks the sensitive skin just below my ear. "Beg for my cock."

"Please, Sebi," I whine, barely recognizing my own cries. "*Please*, I need you inside of me."

He fishes in the nightstand. I grab the condom from him and rip the package with my teeth. His eyes flash, pupils widening—he likes the ferociousness? I can give him that.

I roll the condom on and hook his thighs with my legs. He props himself up and reaches to position his cock at my entrance, but I'm already there, guiding his tip into me, pushing him in with my heels on his ass.

"Quinn," he moans my name.

"Fuck me, Sebi," I beg. I give a heave, and he sheaths into me, all of his cock vanishing into my pussy in one go.

Stars prick the backs of my eyes. He's so *long*—I can feel the whole of him filling up every inch of me, the tip of his cock pounding against the top of my womb.

"Fuck me," I beg again, and he complies.

60

Sebi curls his arms under me, lifting and anchoring, and slams his hips into mine. I cry out; I'd be unable to keep my lips shut even if we were back in that crowd of people. He slams again, again, and I hear him curse into the curve of my neck—

"*Papusa mea*," he says. "*Lubirea mea*."

He isn't speaking in English.

Fuck. Oh my *fuck*. Another orgasm rises just from listening to him come completely apart, unraveling so much he's pushed to speaking in his first language.

"Sebi," I moan his name, "oh my god—"

"Quinn, doll." He brushes his lips over my forehead, his thrusts gaining speed. "You're perfect, *a mea, papusa*—"

I have no idea what he's saying, but it undoes me, and I come with another scream. Sebi is right behind me, his whole body arching and shuddering, eyes rolling shut, mouth parting in a soundless cry.

He collapses on top of me, both of us drenched in sweat and gasping for breath.

"Quinn," he says into my hair. "Stay here tonight. Please. I'll take you to the set in the morning. I can't bear you out of my bed."

"All right," I agree, because my body is utterly spent and I don't think I could walk more than a few feet anyway.

But mostly, I just want to live in this moment of bliss a little longer.

I've had sex before. And fucking him on the dance floor had been the hottest time of my life.

But this? This was transcendent. This was…

Perfect.

So fucking perfect.

And so fucking terrifying.

How will I let this end, knowing how good sex is supposed to be?

He said earlier that I'd wrecked him. I'm starting to think he's wrecked me, too.

CHAPTER EIGHT:
SEBI

Over the next few weeks, Quinn and I fall into a rhythm.

She gets me ready in the makeup trailer; I do whatever scene is on the docket; then I race across set to catch her before she leaves on the crew's hotel bus. Most days I can convince her to come back to my hotel, but other times I beg her to let me take her to dinner, and we find some dive bar or burger joint where the locals have no idea who I am. But we always, always end up in a bed somewhere—hers or mine—or sometimes in an alley behind a restaurant, her body pressed up against the bricks as I plunge my cock into her tight, perfect pussy.

So when another Monday comes around, the film is on schedule, my manager and agent are thrilled I'm only a week out from wrapping and moving onto my planned *big break*, and I get to spend every free minute with the girl of my dreams. Selfishly, I never want this movie to end. I toy with the idea of doing something dramatic to lengthen production, but I'm torn, because I really do *want* that next job.

But I also want Quinn. I want every moment with her, and that wanting is becoming an all-consuming, painful need.

Two days before the movie's scheduled end, Quinn and I get to the makeup trailer ahead of Carmen and the other actors—I wonder if Quinn has realized Carmen is spending a lot of time with the actor who plays my dad, but I don't say anything; good on both of them—and while she sets up, I watch her in the mirror, knowing I'm grinning like a dope.

I have to smile. It distracts me from counting down how much time we have left.

Forty-eight hours.

Quinn sees me watching her. "What, do I have something on my face?" She touches her lips, parting them, and I groan.

"Actually," I start, and a sizzle of eagerness runs up my spine, "I bought you something."

"Sebi." Her tone immediately drops. "Getting dinner together is already enough like a relationship. Gifts—"

64

"It's not that kind of gift. I promise. Purely sex, right?" Wrong. So very wrong. I'm head over heels for this woman, and she knows. It's why she puts such staunch boundaries on our activities together. *We'll get dinner, but only because we both have to eat. I'm paying for myself.*

I pick up the paper bag I'd snagged from my hotel this morning. I know she saw me bring it when we left, but she didn't say anything.

Now, she eyes it, then me in the mirror. With a sigh, she takes it.

I swivel in the chair to clasp her fingers around the top of the bag. "Before you open it, you have to promise me something."

Her eyes flick to mine and I see her lashes flutter with surprise at the earnestness on my face. I'm putting everything I have into the sincerity in which I look at her, my heart well and truly on my sleeve.

I can practically feel her hesitation. "Sebi—"

"Please. Just promise me...that you'll wear it."

Quinn's eyes turn to saucers. I feel her left hand flinch where I'm still holding it.

She thinks it's a ring.

She deserves a ring. A real one. A real one from *me*. I've been swallowing down that desire for the past week, fighting with myself every moment we spend together.

I want to make this girl my wife.

She can't even tolerate the idea of being my girlfriend.

I watch as Quinn reads my expression. "Sebi. Just let me open the bag."

She sounds, if not terrified, then uncertain.

I keep that sincere, pleading expression on my face as I release her hands and she takes a steadying breath.

She opens the bag and slides the box into her hand.

Then she cracks a laugh.

"Oh my *god,* you jerk!" She tosses the empty bag at me. "I was about to pass out. I thought—"

"You thought what?" I'm grinning. I knew she'd think I was giving her a ring— that was the whole point of the game.

But now that she's reacting so intensely to it *not* being a ring…

My smile wavers. I keep it strong, drawing on every acting lesson I've ever had.

Quinn heaves one more relieved breath and refocuses on what *was* in the bag.

66

"What the fuck?" Her laugh is more genuine.

I glance at the door. Carmen still isn't here yet.

"I told you, doll." I take the box from her and dump their contents into my palm. "I want you wearing these."

They're nipple suckers.

Tiny purple suction cups that'll drive her absolutely *wild* with arousal.

Her eyes bulge. "Now?"

"Now."

Quinn's whole face turns red, but she's grinning. "Oh my god. Sebi. Are you out of your mind?"

"Yes. Always, with you. And I want you to be out of your mind today, too."

Because this heaven ends in two days if you choose it.

Because I told you that you'd be in control of this relationship, and I'll stick to that, but I need every memory I can get of what your body looks like utterly sated.

Because the moment this movie wraps, and I lose you, I don't think I'll ever recover.

I stand and walk closer until her back hits the wall of the trailer. Her breathing sharpens, her hands splayed on either side of her body, her breasts rising and falling between us.

She's wearing another sundress—she never wears anything else, and fuck, I love the easy access, the way the material always clings to her curvaceous body—and this one has a square neckline that cuts across her cleavage.

I pinch one of the nipple suckers in my fingers and lick the rim of it. "For suction," I say.

"Ah, you've done this before?"

"There were some…educational videos on the sex toy site."

With my other hand, I tug down her dress, letting a breast pop free.

Whatever quip she'd been about to make—because, yes, I did end up watching a good half hour of porn cleverly disguised as product demonstration videos—gets lost in her sudden wide eyes, the soft purr at the back of her throat.

"Sebi—" She glances behind me, at the closed trailer door.

I kiss her. She moans into me, and as I delve my tongue deep into her mouth, I position the sucker over her already erect nipple, and let it go.

Quinn arches up onto her toes. "Oh fuck. Oh my fuck, Sebi—"

I kiss the side of her mouth. "One more, doll."

68

"Oh my god. How long am I wearing these?"

"All day."

"*All day?* I don't think—"

"I want you writhing for me tonight. I want you so desperate for me that you beg me to spread you wide in the parking lot and take you in front of the entire crew. I want that perfect pussy dripping for me, doll."

I repeat the process with the other sucker. She mewls, whimpering, her whole body shuddering as the nipple suckers tug on what I've learned is one of the most sensitive parts of her body.

Her eyes are dark with desire. My hard cock throbs and it takes a great deal of restraint not to thrust into her right now.

I tuck her beautiful breasts back into her dress and press kisses to the rising mounds of each one. The material is dark blue, hiding the purple suckers, and it kind of just looks like her nipples are erect. No one will know that she's on the edge of orgasm.

Smirking evilly, I brush the nipple suckers through the fabric. "I bet if I touched your clit right now, you'd come, wouldn't you, doll?"

She gulps in a trembling breath. "What are you doing to me?"

That question has been on repeat in my mind for days. *What are you doing to me? I've never felt like this.*

Of course she just means *this* borderline voyeuristic display.

That goddamn pinch in my stomach needs to fucking go *away*. I will enjoy these last few hours with her, and I will *not* think about how soon it all ends.

The door opens behind us.

"Good morning, you two," Carmen mumbles as she bangs inside, dark shades hiding that she was likely out late last night. She goes to her station without another word, gulping from a giant cup of coffee.

I sit back down, and fuck me, I have to readjust twice to hide my boner. Quinn goes to the makeup cart—stumbles, more like— and braces her hands on the edges to take one full, deep breath before she picks up her notes on today's look.

She sets them down.

Picks them up again.

Sets them down.

"Fuck, Sebi, I can't even think," she giggle-whispers to the makeup cart.

70

I bite down on my lip. I'm so aware of how we're not alone anymore, and it both drives me wild and makes me want to scream at Carmen to leave so I can fuck Quinn's brains out.

As Quinn finally grabs the first product and turns to me, I shift my shoulder, brushing one of the nipple suckers.

Quinn chirps.

Carmen gives her a *what the fuck* look. "You cut yourself?"

"No. N-no. I'm fine." Quinn starts brushing something on my face. "Totally fucking fine."

She says the last part low, a growl at me.

"Stop smiling," she chastises me.

"Not gonna happen." I run my fingers along the edge of her thigh where it rests against my chair. A dip to the side, and my fingers barely brush her panties.

They're *drenched.*

Oh my god, I'm gonna blow in my pants.

"This is torture for us both, just so you know," I tell her, letting her hear the hot desire in my tone.

Quinn's breathing is raspy. She switches products and instead of gently tipping my head back like she usually does, her fingers wrap around my throat and thrust my face up.

Oh *Christ*.

I hiss, eyes snapping shut, digging deep for resolve not to come untouched.

"Quinn," I groan.

She doesn't say anything. Her hand slides off my neck and she gets back to work, and when I look up at her, her eyes are still dark, her cheeks flushed, her lips in a flat line.

I know that frustrated look—she's fighting hard not to come.

Oh, tonight is going to be *fun*.

Fun enough that she gives in and lets me be part of her life after this movie?

I rub my chest, willing the thought away, focusing only on the crease between her brows and the intoxicating way she has to keep stopping what she's doing to catch her breath through her arousal.

CHAPTER NINE: QUINN

Finally, *finally,* the day wraps.

The moment we get the alert, I tear out of the makeup trailer. Carmen laughs as I go; she has no idea why I was so squirmy all day, but I'm sure she suspects it's something to do with who I've spent literally every night with. It really is becoming a problem—we only have one more day of shooting, one more day of whatever it is Sebi and I are doing. I keep waiting for him to get bored with me and stop coming around at the end of the day; I keep waiting for him to do or say something that reminds me why I don't date actors.

It hasn't happened yet. Impossibly.

And now, I can't even think through my blind pulse of desire. Sebi wanted to drive me crazy? Oh, he *succeeded*. He more than succeeded. My vision is entirely scarlet. I can feel my pulse in the tips of my fingers, in the hard bud of my clit, in each tortured nipple. My whole body trembles with need for release as I cut across the parking lot to Sebi's trailer.

I clamber inside. He isn't here yet—he always comes here, changes, then usually races across the lot to meet me—and I let out a pained groan in the empty space.

Not a beat later, the door rattles behind me, and Sebi climbs in.

He pulls back, startled, but his face relaxes when he sees me. He takes in my expression—teeth bared, shoulders heaving, already a little sweaty—and he grins like he's so goddamn *satisfied* with himself.

Fuck, I hate him.

I hate him so much that my whole body responds in kind, arousal peaking at the mere sight of him, a strangled whimper catching in my throat.

I hate him because I don't hate him yet. I hate that this *hurts*—not just my arousal, but being with him, because it hasn't gone sour yet, and we're both leaving after tomorrow and my chest aches at the thought of not seeing him every day.

"Need something, doll?" Sebi asks, stepping closer to me.

I dive at him. My mouth clamps to his, the kiss brutal and bruising, punishment for what he's put me through today. He immediately matches my intensity, biting my bottom lip as his hands grab the straps of my dress and yank down.

74

My abused breasts pop free and I arch back with a moan. "Sebi, *please*."

"Shh, doll, I got you." He kiss-bites his way down my neck, pain and pleasure. "Take a deep breath."

I comply.

Off comes one nipple sucker.

I scream, pain flaring, but also—fuck, *fuck*, nothing has ever felt so amazing, every nerve ending in my nipple absolutely raw and spasming, and then Sebi's mouth is on it, sucking gently, his tongue running tender laps around the pebbled nub.

The noises I'm making aren't even human. Blubbers and begs and mewls.

He kisses his way to my other breast and I brace, whimpering already. The sucker comes off in another perfect, destructive mix of euphoria and agony that has my whole body bucking in Sebi's arms.

He keeps a tight grip around my waist as his tongue nurses the other nipple, prodding deep at it, and when he shifts to simultaneously rub the first nipple against the pad of his hand, I come.

I come so hard and so fast that my body goes completely limp. Sebi swings me to lay out across his couch, the orgasm tearing through me in building waves—first one, damaging, beautiful, spotting my vision black; then another, stronger somehow, and I feel Sebi's fingers on my clit and the sudden, filling push of his cock gliding into me; then a third wave, cresting high as Sebi pumps into me, all of my most sensitive places turned on and cranked to the max.

Tears pour down my face. Sweat too. I'm whimpering and moaning and sobbing as I cling to him, riding this high into the unknown, helpless not to get swept away in the sensation, in this wonderful man who knows my body so intimately that he brought me beyond orgasm, to a space of utter bliss.

"Quinn," he moans my name into my hair. "Quinn—"

He comes, shouting into the couch cushion, his body rippling against mine as my own orgasms subside and leave me gasping for air. I can't catch my breath. I can't see. I can only feel—Sebi's body falling against mine. Him rolling to the side, clinging me to him, and me draping my limbs around him. My body tingling head to toe, breasts so sensitive that when they rub against his chest, I cry out, and Sebi flinches, murmuring *I'm sorry, doll,* before he showers them in fluttering kisses.

I may never move again. I may just die here, in his arms, one hundred percent content.

76

Eventually, Sebi gets me to my feet.

"Shower, doll," he tells me.

"Is it big enough for us both?"

He smirks and kisses my nose. "We'll make do. But keep your hands to yourself, Quinn—I think that beautiful body of yours needs a rest."

Hardly. I'm exhausted and sated but as he steps away to dip into the little bathroom compartment, I find myself reaching after him.

This whole situation is in my control. If I want to keep seeing him after this movie, I can—I just need to tell him. He set this stipulation.

Did he mean it?

Wouldn't things change after this movie? I'll be wherever I get assigned next; he's off to some other film most likely. This is where it gets hard. So why ruin what we have with trying to make it about something other than amazing sex?

I shiver, realizing that sometime in my ecstasy, he stripped me naked. As I turn to grab a blanket from the couch, the shower kicks on.

My eyes catch on a script on his end table.

I wrap in the fluffy blanket—it smells like him; fuck, maybe he'll let me keep this—and pull the script into my hands.

Why do I recognize the title? This has to be his next project. Did he mention it to me? Do I—

I flip to the page that lists the principal cast.

And my whole body goes still.

"Water's warm, doll." Sebi comes out of the bathroom.

I can't get my mouth to move for a full breath. By the time I look up at Sebi, his brows are furrowed.

"What's wrong?" He takes the script from me, looks it over, decides nothing's amiss, and drops it onto the table.

Of course he wouldn't know. Would he? Didn't he read the articles? Didn't he see the tabloids? *Everyone* saw the tabloids.

"That movie," I say, my mouth dry. "Your co-star."

"Chris Griffins? What about him?" Sebi smiles, but it's tight; he can tell I'm worried, but can't place why. "If you're worried I'll fall for him and forget you, don't. He's not my type. And, actually, I wanted to talk to you about that. About…us. After."

"Not him." I can't let him keep talking. Can't let this go. "The other co-star. Garth Daniels."

"Yeah?" Sebi cocks his head.

"Have you worked with him before?"

"No? I barely know him." It comes out as a question, Sebi's head still cocked. "Quinn, what's this about? What are you—"

He stops.

His eyes go wide.

"Oh, *shit*." He puts a hand to his mouth and winces in a way I've seen so many fucking times. People realizing that I'm *that* Quinn McGill. That I'm *that* ex-wife who was seduced, married, and divorced in less than three months.

"My ex-husband," I say, eyes on the script.

Sebi's next movie is with my ex-husband.

I don't know why it bothers me. It shouldn't bother me.

But all I can imagine, suddenly, are Sebi and Garth laughing in their trailers, comparing notes about my body.

"Quinn." Sebi scrubs his hand over his face. "I won't be able to look at the guy without decking him for you."

I shudder, pulling the blanket more tightly around me. "It's fine."

"The fuck it is, Quinn!" His hands drop. His face goes slack. "I'll pull out of the movie."

I flinch a full step back from him. "You will not. Do you hear yourself?"

"I do. Doll—" He reaches for me, but I keep my hands in the blanket; he settles for grabbing my shoulders, his thumbs pressing against the blanket's fluff. "You're in control still. You always will be. But you should know that I'm absolutely wild about you, and—"

"*Stop*." I twist away from him and drop the blanket onto the couch. There are my panties, my dress; I tug them on with shaking hands. "You don't mean this. If you drop this movie because of me, you'll come to resent me. I won't let you."

"Then—then what do we do?" Sebi steps in front of me. Between me and the door, I realize.

I smooth my hair back, sure I look a mess. I *feel* a mess suddenly, all my insides that were so recently twisted in rapture now spinning in dread.

I knew it was too good to be true.

I *knew* it would get to this moment. Didn't I fucking know? This is why I don't date actors. This is why I wear that ring. *This is why*.

80

Because this is killing me.

Looking into his eyes. Seeing the anxiety stretching his features, his sexy, naked body wound like he wants to leap to our defense, only he can't.

"We leave tomorrow," I tell him, and it comes out soft, because I can't bear to say it any louder. "Just like we always were going to."

"If I do this movie with your ex, can I still see you? I'll come to wherever you are after the shoot wraps. I'll—"

"No, Sebastian."

He stops, jaw snapping shut.

"This is it, okay? I told you this is all I can handle." My heart thuds, too fast, too heavy. Tears prick the backs of my eyes. I need to say this and *leave*. I need to get out of this trailer. "This was never a relationship."

Even if he's the kindest, most empathetic, most patient man I've ever met. Even if every part of my body cries out for him in a way I've never even begun to feel for anyone, least of all Garth.

I force myself to close the space between us and kiss Sebi on the cheek.

"I'll see you tomorrow morning," I say into the bend of his neck.

His hands plant on my waist. "Quinn." It's begging. Full of sorrow and a million words he wants to say but won't because *he* gave me control, and he still, even now, isn't taking it back.

I love him.

Oh my god.

I love this man.

This was *not* supposed to happen ever again.

I shove around Sebi and burst out of the trailer.

I'm sobbing by the time I get back to the hotel. Carmen's in bed, propped up with a book and a glass of wine.

She takes one look at me and I spend the rest of the night curled next to her, alternating between crying and drinking. And in the morning, she pats my head, tells me she'll cover for me, and heads to the set.

I should go. I should say goodbye, one last time.

But I just burrow under the blankets and wait for the pain in my chest to go numb.

It never does.

CHAPTER TEN:
SEBI

"Hi! I'm Stacey—I'll be your makeup artist for this film."

I barely hear her. I have one earbud in, where I've been listening to a playlist I've named *Heartbreak can kiss my ass* on loop since last Friday. Pathetic? Hell yes I'm pathetic.

All I can manage is a nod at the new girl—Stacey? And she gives a halfhearted smile like she's already thinking *Great, another self-absorbed actor.*

Which was exactly what Quinn thought, wasn't it? And that's exactly what I am. Because I didn't fucking hesitate to come to this big shoot. I didn't chase after her even when Carmen said she was sick that final day. I didn't text her or check in on her—because I was gutted. And I didn't want to show up at her hotel room as a blubbering mess. Who would've taken *that* seriously?

Besides, she made her choice.

I have to respect it.

83

I close my eyes as Stacey gets to work. Day one of this film. This film that could make or break my whole damn career. I should switch to a more pump-it-up playlist, but every time I start to, I see the song Quinn and I fucked to in the dance club. I feel her tight body pressed to mine. I hear the little noises she'd make, moans and squeals, and *fuck*.

Am I crying? God, not now.

I sniff. "Stacey, give me a sec, would you? I need some air."

I don't wait to see if she agrees—it's suddenly way too claustrophobic in here. The smell of the makeup and hair supplies. The sound of Stacey's heels on the tile just like Quinn's.

Fuck. *Fuck*.

I shove outside. It's barely dawn. Thank god this first part of shooting is in LA, not abroad; I'd be an absolute disaster with jet lag thrown in. I stand for a second in the not-quite-silence, listening to the crew bustling around while my playlist switches tracks to *Hallelujah* by Hannah Trigwell. The first mournful notes peel into my other ear and I wince, but it's good. This is part of healing, right? This is—

A shoulder jostles mine.

I look up, and the world goes red.

"Sebastian Stanik, right?" asks Garth Daniels.

I've met the entire rest of the cast except for Garth, who's such a big shot that he didn't need to show up for anything until the exact moment he's needed to film. Today.

My jaw dips open. I pull my earbud out and my fingers curl into fists by my sides when I realize his hand is out for a shake.

I run my tongue over my teeth. "Garth."

He waits a beat then lets his hand drop. His demeanor immediately changes, rising to the unspoken challenge, and god—is that a glimmer of a smile on his face? He likes this macho shit.

"Been hearing a lot about you," Garth tells me, his smile tight. "You just wrapped some romantic comedy?"

He says *romantic comedy* like I was stepping in dog shit.

"Yeah." And because defensive is rising up in me like a vicious tidal wave, I add, "I met your ex-wife."

Garth's eyebrows shoot up. I can see his mind working. *Which one?*

Fuck, I hate this guy. Like *achingly* hate this guy.

"Quinn McGill," I clarify.

85

Garth laughs. "Ah. *Her*. She's a spitfire, eh? Still got that fine body?"

It takes a great deal of restraint not to hit him. "She's great, actually. Amazing. You really messed up letting that one go."

Garth's smile goes savage. "You fucked her, didn't you?"

Shit. Though, honestly, I don't care if he knows. I kind of *want* him to know just so he can wallow in how much happier I made her.

But I didn't make her happier, did I?

Shit. Don't think about that. Not now.

Garth bends closer, his eyes alight, his lips in a sneer. "I tried to whip her into shape, but she's a lousy lay, isn't she?"

I blink.

And Garth is on the ground.

My hand stings.

Oh, fuck.

Oh fuck *oh fuck*.

I punched him.

Instantly, crewmembers rush us, but Garth's already climbing to his feet, one hand on his jaw. I'm gasping, every muscle wound, ready to run or defend myself—I can't really tell what that look in his eyes means.

He spits a wad of blood to the side and gives me a bloody smile.

He *is* enjoying this. The sick bastard loves these mental games.

"Nice to meet you, Stanik," is all he says before he shoves aside the fluttering crewmembers and climbs into the makeup trailer.

I stand there, ignoring the people asking me what happened.

What happened is I punched my girl's ex-husband.

But she isn't even *my girl*.

And isn't that just *stupid?*

Why didn't I fight for her? Why am I so eager and willing to punch out creeps on her behalf, but when it came to fighting for *us,* I just…walked away?

I turn and race across the lot for my own trailer. Halfway there, I'm tearing my phone out of my pocket and dialing my manager.

He and my agent are going to flip shit. But I can't stay here. Not like this. Not without my doll.

CHAPTER ELEVEN: QUINN

I put the finishing touches on my lipstick. "Car, you ready? The correct answer is *yes*."

She shouts something indistinct from my back bathroom.

"I'll take that as a no." I sigh and drop to sit on my couch, trying not to wrinkle my ivory club dress.

It's nice that my next assignment is in LA and I get to sleep in my own bed, but honestly, I'd have preferred another traveling gig. I want to be going, doing, *moving* to keep my mind off of how Sebi is in the same town as me, filming his big blockbuster with Garth.

Hence the midweek club date with Carmen.

I shouldn't care. I *can't* care. I chose this, remember? I chose to end us because it would fucking hurt too much to watch him eventually choose his career over me. So *I* chose me.

And it sucks.

Epically.

The doorbell rings.

88

"Carmen!" I shout. "Our ride's here!" But they don't usually come to the door— they let me know on the app.

Confusion has me looking down at my phone as I cross the living room to answer.

"Is there something wrong with—"

My question dies flat in my throat.

Sebi stands on my doorstep, a giant bundle of roses in one hand and a look of breathless panic on his face.

All logic and sense completely evaporate from my body.

I shake my head. "You—how did you know where I live?"

He blushes. Fuck, that's still adorable. "I pulled some strings."

"Creepy."

"Yes. But I'm desperate. You make me desperate, Quinn."

My stomach cinches tight. "Sebastian—"

"Just let me talk first, please?"

I relent, only because my throat is swelling shut, and I don't want to cry, I *won't* cry.

"Quinn," he starts, and *fuck me* his voice sounds pinched too, "I'm sorry I didn't fight for us. You deserve someone who will fight for *you,* for our relationship, and at the first test of that, I failed. But I won't fail again if you give me a chance. Every time it's in my control, I'll put you first. I want to be with you, not just as a fling, but in a real, true relationship. I love you, Quinn McGill."

He stops, panting, his cheeks as red as the roses.

There's a long beat of silence. I can't make myself draw a breath. I'm supposed to be doing something, right? Talking or reacting in some way.

But all I can get out is, "Your movie."

Sebi shrugs. "It'll wait. It'll always wait for me to make things right with you."

Tears finally make their way down my cheeks. I sob once, hard, and it rocks me forward, into Sebi's arms.

He catches me, the flowers crashing to the ground, and I knot my arms around his neck. God, it's only been a few days, but it feels like a lifetime, a lifetime I thought I wouldn't get, a lifetime I really, really want.

"I love you too," I whisper into his cheek, kissing his ear, his jaw, working my way around to his perfect, smiling lips.

"God, doll, I missed you so much," he says into my mouth. "Fuck, I'm sorry."

90

"Don't apologize. I shouldn't have left like that." I twine my legs around his waist as he walks us backwards, into my apartment. "I was so scared, Sebi. But I realize now that I'm *not* scared. Not with you."

I feel his smile against mine. "Say that again."

"I'm not scared, not with—"

"No. My name."

I giggle. "Sebi."

He grabs my ass, growling into another kiss that ricochets straight to my pussy. My whole body missed him too, and it lights up now, preening under his touch.

He goes still. "There is something you should probably know, though."

I pull back enough to look at him.

"I punched Garth," he says, his lips in a straight line like he's fighting a smile.

My eyes go wide.

Then I laugh.

I laugh so hard that Sebi rocks a little, adjusting me, and our lips meet again, the two of us giggling helplessly.

A throat clears.

Sebi and I turn to see Carmen in my kitchen, popping Cheetos into her mouth.

She gives us a shitty grin. "I guess the girl's night is off?"

"Oh no," Sebi says the same moment I say, "Yes."

I whip to look at him, still in his arms, still feeling his rock hard cock through his jeans where it presses directly against my slit.

"Sebi," I say his name almost chastising.

He just grins and nips at my mouth. "You're going dancing, right? If you remember, I'm quite the excellent dancer."

That makes my whole body spasm in a warm wave.

I somehow manage to look away from him, at Carmen again. "Do you mind if Sebi comes?"

She wrinkles her nose at me in a grin. "Gives me an excuse to invite my guy too."

"Your guy?" My eyes widen. She'd mentioned Sebi's co-star a few times, but never anything serious.

Carmen whips out her phone and punches a text. "Double date?"

"Double date." Sebi bites my ear and I arch against him. "But the things I'm going to do to you on the dance floor will be just for us," he whispers to me.

Just for us...and the dozens of other people thrashing around us to whatever violent techno song is playing.

I bend against Sebi, kissing him with everything I have in me, everything he's willing to hold onto.

CHAPTER TWELVE: QUINN

Six Months Later

I *adore* the setting for Sebi's latest movie. A small indie flick set on the Atlantic coast, complete with loads of idyllic lighthouses and sandy shores. Every time I step outside, the smell of saltwater perfumes the air, and I immediately relax.

A soft, warm breeze ruffles my hair where I stand just next to the makeup trailer, head tipped back, sun on my face.

Arms come around my waist. "Sorry I'm late, doll. Scene ran long."

I lean back into him, and the feeling of relaxation only deepens. Since Sebi wrapped on his big blockbuster movie and it's still projected to do insanely well, he's been able to request me as his personal makeup artist on his other films. So, in an insane twist for Hollywood, we're actually maintaining a

94

healthy relationship where we see each other every day and share a hotel room. Enhance it all with working together, too, and I'm shocked we haven't gotten sick of each other yet.

The opposite, in fact—the more time I spend with this man, the more in love I fall.

I spin in his arms and press a kiss to his lips. "Ready to go? I'm starving. The director recommended a seafood place on a pier that we have to try."

But as I step away, Sebi grabs my hand and winces. "Actually, I think I left something in the makeup trailer. Can we run in and grab it really quick first?"

"Oh. Sure." My stomach rumbles, but I follow him up the steps.

The other artist and I—not Carmen, who is back in LA with her own remarkably stable boyfriend—cleaned and locked up an hour ago, so Sebi plods in as I flick on the light.

Instead of searching for anything, he drops into his usual chair.

And just sits there.

"Um. What is it you left here?" I cast my gaze over the room as I walk closer to him, but I already know there was nothing out of place when we cleaned up.

Sebi fishes something out of his pocket and holds up a small paper bag.

My body goes hot. I stop behind him, holding his eyes in the mirror.

"Sebi, is that…" my voice trails off, desire choking my words. He's pulled out the nipple suckers a few times—okay, more than a few times—but to wear them during dinner will be a special kind of torture.

He just holds out the bag, grinning, his eyes sparkling.

I take it and pull out the contents. A new box of nipple suckers stares up at me and I cut him a giddy smirk in the mirror as I pop the lid.

"Sebastian Stanik," I say, naughty, "you know what this does to—"

I stop.

My hand feels what fell out of the box before the rest of my body makes sense of it. Not nipple suckers. Something hard and circular. Something—

I look down at the ring in my hand.

When I look back up, Sebi is on his knees before me, his eyes tearing.

"Quinn McGill," he starts, his lips trembling. He licks them, smiles, fighting for composure, and it reminds me to breathe, deep breaths, in and out. "Quinn. I love you, and I want to spend the rest of my life showing you just how much. Will you marry me?"

He clicks a button in his pocket and the whole trailer starts to play a song. *Our* song, the one from the dance club. It's not even remotely a romance song but it instantly makes me think of him, of us, and my already teary eyes overflow.

"Are you sure?" I squeak out.

"Yes." He smiles up at me. "I've never been more sure of anything, doll."

So I nod. And again. And then he's standing, wrapping me in his arms as I slide the ring on my finger. A *real* ring now, not one used to deter men, not one ripe with memories of a failed marriage.

"You're going to marry me," I say, because I'm half stunned with shock and also giggling like a little girl.

Sebi kisses my neck and holds me to him. "I am, doll. I'm going to marry the shit out of you."

I laugh. Our song builds to the breaking point and Sebi slides me on the counter, kissing all the way down my neck to the bend of my breast. He pulls my shirt down and frees a breast to lightly kiss my nipple, making me moan and writhe, my fingers fumbling at his own shirt.

"Make love to me, Sebi," I beg him. "Please."

His eyes are dark, heady with desire and happiness and all the emotions swirling in me too. As I pull his zipper down and free his cock, he lifts the hem of my skirt and dives his fingers straight into my pussy. He already knows I'm not wearing panties—it drives him crazy in my sundresses and skirts.

This is why. Easy access, so all he has to do is hike my hips closer to the edge of the counter. The size of him never fails to take my breath away, filling me completely, his rock hard dick slamming on my walls and building sensation with each jarring movement.

He thrusts into me as our song blares around us and his ring glints on my finger.

THE END

For more sizzling celebrity fantasies brought to life, check out the two other books in the *Celebrity Crush* series:

MEET CUTE: When a production company sets their next biopic on the tiny island of Havensboro, global heartthrob Tom Hudel sneaks ashore early to do some research…and that *research* takes a sexy turn when he meets a local waitress who agrees to be his tour guide.

OFF CAMERA: A PR intern accepts an unorthodox assignment to be Hollywood bad boy Chris Griffin's faux-girlfriend—and gets far more than she bargained for…

Stay up-to-date on any releases from Natasha Luxe, join her shared newsletter with Liza Penn! You'll get double the spicy reads for one easy sign up. (But don't worry, we won't spam you—max two emails a month!)

https://rarebooks.substack.com/welcome

Read on for an exclusive excerpt from Celebrity Crush: MEET CUTE!

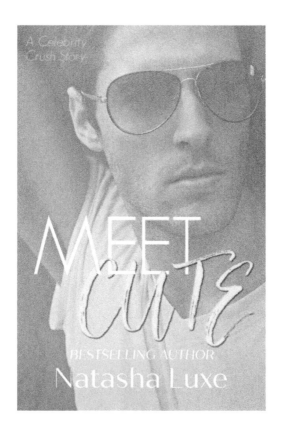

He hovers his lips on top of mine. His fingers are working at the other strap of my overalls. A click, a slither, and it falls off.

"I want to taste of all you," he tells me, and my knees weaken. "You deserve a proper thank you, after all."

Yes, yes, I do. I don't even know what I'm really agreeing to, just that I need more of him, more of *this*. Each touch sets fire to the chemistry we'd had in the diner, electricity ramped all the way up, explosion imminent. Every spark of his touch on my skin sizzles through me; his eyes on my body makes me feel impossibly sexy, some kind of goddess of sin and salvation come to life before him.

I want whatever he has to offer.

I want it all.

My overalls are already hanging on just to my hips. I push them the rest of the way down my body, letting them pool around my ankles. I'm left in just my pink tank top, one breast hanging out, and Tom sees now that I'm not wearing any panties.

His eyes bulge. He teeters, catching himself on the wall by my head. "Darling, what you do to me."

"The better question," I pant, "is what are you going to do to me?"

He growls. Lips curling up, eyes all pupil, absolutely vicious, and I feel a surge between my legs, wetness, ready for him.

He doesn't rip open his pants, though.

Tom drops to his knees, running his hands down my body, pulling the other strap of my tank top and bra down as he goes. My shirt and bra bunches around my waist and he fills each hand with a breast, kneading, rolling his palms over my nipples as he lowers his face to my pussy.

"Tom," I gasp his name, and he blows gently on the sensitive skin above my thighs.

His hands slip off my breasts to trickle down, grabbing one thigh, sliding it to the side. He has a full view of me; he can see my wetness, my eagerness for him.

"So wet," he says and slides a finger down my folds. He pushes it in and I whine, biting down the noise in my throat. "So wet for me."

He pulls his finger out, the tip glistening with moisture, and slides it into his mouth the same way I licked the whipped cream from my thumb. Indulgently, his eyes rolling shut, a low moan echoing in his throat.

He doesn't say anything else. He leans in and strokes long licks through my folds like each taste makes him hungry for more. I can hear him moaning with pleasure as much I hear my own moans, our pleasure mingling as we fight and fail to keep it quiet.

My body bucks against the wall with each expert lick he gives me, that vicious tongue sliding up, swirling around my clit, diving back down. He traces every inch of me, leaving nothing untouched until I'm vibrating with building need.

"Tom—I'm so close, please—"

He moans his assent. Those lips land on my clit, kissing deeply, before he sucks in, pulling my clit into his mouth.

I scream into my lips, keening like a madwoman. The orgasm tears at every nerve in fireworks that will incinerate me inside out, but I don't care, let it burn me, let me fall apart here and now. He keeps sucking through my climax, dragging every ounce of pleasure from my twitching clit, until my stifled screams turn to whimpers.

He hauls himself back up my body, kissing each nipple, my neck, my cheeks. He curls his arms around me and I go limp against him, sweat sheening my skin, my breaths coming in gasping breaths.

104

"Avery," he says my name into my mouth, and I kiss him, tasting myself on him. And fuck, that just ignites me even more—I need this man inside of me, need him more fiercely than I've ever felt—

"You have a room here?" I gasp.

He grins against me. I feel his lips lift. "Yes. 211."

"Go. Let's go." I scramble out of his arms and roughly tug on my overalls, tucking myself back into my bra and tank top.

He chuckles but catches my wrist as I dart past him for the door. I swing on him and he grabs the back of my neck, cradling my head in the museum's low light.

The pause reorients me, helps me see through my fog of desire.

There's something on his face now, a pinch to his brows, a gravity in his eyes.

"Avery," he says my name again. God, I don't think I'll ever get tired of the way he says it. "There is nothing I would like more than to throw you on my bed and continue showing that body just how quickly I am becoming obsessed with you, but I have to tell you something first."

I go still. "Oh god, you're married?"

He smiles. "No. Far from it. Perpetually single, the tabloids say."

Tabloids?

105

Why would tabloids care about a movie producer?

My mind trips.

He *is* a producer. Isn't he?

I stare at him, this time, analytically.

Those green eyes. That chiseled jaw. That smile that I've seen on magazine covers and late night interviews and in a dozen movies—

My eyes fly all the way open.

Oh my god.

I'd thought I'd recognized him. But why the *fuck* would *he* be on this island early, and alone, and so unabashedly flirting with a small-town waitress? No. No *way*.

"I'm Tom Hudel," he tells me. His smile is kind of sad, but I refuse to let it get to me. "As in…"

"*Tom Hudel*," I repeat.

Printed in Great Britain
by Amazon